TONIA the TREE

Written by **Sandy Stryker**

Illustrated by **Itoko Maeno**

Advocacy Press • Santa Barbara

For
Mindy

Text Copyright © 1988 by Sandy Stryker
Illustration Copyright © 1988 by Itoko Maeno

Published by Advocacy Press
P.O. Box 236
Santa Barbara, California 93102 USA

*Advocacy Press is a division of the Girls Club of Santa Barbara, an affiliate
of Girls Clubs of America, Inc.*

Library of Congress Cataloging-in-Publication Data

Stryker, Sandy.
  Tonia the tree.

  Summary: Tonia the tree fears that change is part of growing and living
and should not be feared.
[1. Trees—Fiction. 2 Conduct of life—Fiction. 3. Fear—Fiction. 4. Story is
in rhyme] I. Maeno, Itoko, ill. II. Title.
PZ8.3.S915To 1988   [E]   88-16769

ISBN 0-911655-16-6

Printed in Hong Kong

Tonia the Tree had a wonderful life
In the forest of Higgledy-boo.
In the night she spread breezes, in the day she spread shade,
And all through the year, Tonia grew.

Liggledy Birds made a home in her hair
Out of string, beeble grass and warm clay.
Wiggledy Worms crawled around Tonia's toes
And taught her the games that they play.

With work, fun, and friends, Tonia had a full life
And for years she continued to grow.
At first she grew fast, but as the years passed,
Tonia's growth lost its pace and grew slow.

Her leaves, once so green, took on a grey cast;
Her arms seemed to sag in all weather.
Instead of warm dirt, her toes struck hard rock
And soon her growth stopped altogether.

No one could say as a certainty when
This cessation of growth had occurred.
"Two years this Christmas," the Wiggle Worms said.
"Oh no, it was spring," said the birds.

Tonia's companions did little at first
But wear sad, worried looks on their face.
Some brought her fresh water and felt her warm trunk,
While others just felt out of place.

"Sick trees need special attention," one said.
"There's only so much we can do.
If Tonia has really stopped growing, I think
We should call the tree surgeon, don't you?"

Reluctantly, then, the others agreed.
A tree that won't grow must be sick.
They got on the Higgledy-Grapevine and said,
"Send the tree surgeon, please, and be quick."

The doctor arrived with a satchel of tools
And set out to see what was wrong.
She checked Tonia's tonsils and looked at her leaves
As she whistled a tree surgeon's song.

She listened and tinkered and looked at the tree
From all angles and every position.
Then she announced, "What she needs is a change.
It's as sure as is I'm a physician.

"The soil here just can't meet her needs any more.
And she's not learning anything new.
It's not that this tree doesn't love all you folks,
But there's not enough for her to do.

"I know just the place for our Tonia,
A space where she really can grow.
She'll become a tree we can be proud of,
A tree we'll be pleased that we know."

"Oh, no," cried out Tonia, "don't move me.
I can grow *here* on this spot
If I just make my mind up to do it.
You go on. I'll stay here. Thanks a lot.

"Maybe I just need a trimming,
Or a new coat of wax on my leaves.
I could hang some new nests from my branches,
Or tuck my arms into new sleeves."

The tree surgeon gazed at her patient.
"You're sick, but I know you're not dim.
You know growth doesn't come from the outside.
Growth only comes from within."

"But trees *can't* be moved," replied Tonia.
"I know that it's never been done!
We're too big. We're too old. We're too set in our ways.
We're just sticks in the mud, everyone!"

"You're much more than a stick," said the doctor.
"You have roots, you have leaves, you can grow.
You're alive, and that means you have options.
Trees can move. Trees can change. This I know."

The Liggledy Birds had been listening
And tried to ease Tonia's fear.
"We change all the time," they told Tonia.
"It's great fun to fly south every year."

"Oh, it's easy for you," Tonia told them.
"You have feet. You have wings. You can fly.
For *me* change means being uprooted!
It's a *gamble,* a *risk.* I could *die*!"

"We weren't born in mid-air," the birds answered.
"Once *we* were helpless like you.
Our moms and our dads had to feed us
In the nests where we sat dumb and new.

"It wasn't exactly exciting
To sit at the top of a tree
With a nest full of brothers and sisters,
Though it was safer than just being free.

"But our parents were having none of it.
They *insisted* we learn how to fly.
They *taught* us, of course, how to do it.
When we *learned* it was 'Birdy, bye-bye.'"

"Are you saying that you, too, were frightened?"
The tree found this hard to believe.
The birds made it all look so easy.
Could she really have been that naive?

"No one finds change is that simple,"
The birds then proceeded to say.
"Feeling the fear is quite natural,
But you just have to change anyway."

"Okay," Tonia said. "Then I'll do it.
I'll take a deep breath and I'll go.
It's all right, Doc, you have my permission.
It's once again time that I grow."

The very next morning it happened.
The tree surgeon came before dawn
With her higa-mejiggle machinery
And a truck to put Tonia on.

"You'll soon feel much better," she promised
As she dug all around in the dirt.
"Be a brave tree. We'll all help you.
I promise it really won't hurt."

All the trees in the forest stood silent
As the truck carrying Tonia passed.
Would it work? Could she grow? Oh, they hoped so!
She *must* resume growing at last!

Before Tonia knew what had happened,
The truck slowly came to a stop.
"This is it, your new home," said the doctor.
"You'll live here, on the hill. Near the top."

"It's a beautiful site," she admitted.
"Maybe this won't be so bad."
Then she wriggled her toes in excitement
And the birds thought she grew . . . just a tad.

The sun had come out now to greet her,
And help Tonia know she belonged.
And at night there was rain touched with stardust
To help the weak tree become strong.

The air on the hill was a tonic.
Tonia had to admit it was so.
She loved how it made her arms jiggle
While her feet remained anchored below.

Soon Tonia felt something happen—
Something vaguely familiar, yet new.
"New leaves," cried the birds. "Hey, you're growing!"
Tonia laughed, then she looked. It was true!

As she dug her toes deep in the soil,
Tonia flung her long arms toward the sun.
Once more the tree seemed to be changing
And she cried, "Look at me! This is fun!"

"Well," said the birds who'd stayed with her,
"If you don't mind, we'll be moving along.
We're due to fly south," they told Tonia.
Tonia smiled and said "thanks." They were gone.

Then in silent salute to her comrades
Who had taught her so much, Tonia turned
Her leaves red, fiery orange and bright yellow
To show just how much she had learned.

Other trees on the hill looked at Tonia.
"Oh, how pretty, how lovely," they said.
"Green is a nice enough color,
But how grand for a tree to be red!"

Soon all the trees began changing
And the hill turned a rainbow of leaves.
Leaves of red, leaves of orange, leaves of yellow—
What bright patterns a hillside can weave!

That, though, was just the beginning.
Next Tonia decided to shed
Her jacket of multiple colors
To be used on the ground as a bed

For the Wiggledy Worms who were weary,
For the bumbles and beetles to nest.
Then all through the winter she stood there
To take a well-earned woody rest.

In the spring when the sun became warmer
And new life poked its head from the ground,
Tonia's limbs began bursting with blossoms
That launched sweet perfume skyward bound.

The scent soon attracted attention
To the tree with such beauty to lend.
Other creatures came 'round just to see her,
And most of them stayed to be friends.

"How could anyone fail to love Tonia,"
A friend in the forest reflects.
"She's so brave and so smart and creative.
You never know what she'll do next!"

"Till she came around, life was boring.
We all did the same dead, dull things.
Tonia's change has been our inspiration.
What once was a worm now has wings!

Raindrops adopted new patterns.

Flowers have turned into fruit.
Even the tiniest seeds in the ground
Are shoving out confident shoots.

Now all through the forest where once little changed,
Change has become a tradition.
Growth is encouraged, new goals are pursued,
And dreams are all brought to fruition.

"Don't be frightened of change," Tonia says now.
"Change is what helps you to grow.
It makes for a life of adventure.
            Just ask me.
                    I'll tell you.
                            I should know."

The concept of change must be examined like a two-faced coin. While one side reflects its *inevitability,* the other reminds us of its *possibility.* Children must learn to deal with the former if they are to survive. And they must embrace the latter if they are to dream and prosper.

Essential as it is, the ability to cope with—or even thrive on—change is a skill not often or easily taught. Perhaps the only way to master it is with practice. For better or worse, most children have ample opportunity to deal with change:

- A baby brother or sister arrives
- A parent who has been at home gets an outside job
- A grandparent dies
- Parents change or lose jobs
- Parents divorce or remarry
- Families relocate and children face new schools, new friends

Sometimes they even seek *change* out:

- An "awkward" child wants to take up basketball or ballet
- A "slow reader" wants to read the classics
- A student not previously interested in math or science is intrigued by the new class computer

All children deal constantly with the traumas of growing, learning and living with others. Parents and teachers can help by showing children that change is not only normal and inescapable, but a source of excitement and adventure.

Some ways to do this:

- Discuss Tonia's story. Why was she afraid of change? How did she overcome her fear? Was she better off before or after her move? How did her courage affect others? What might have happened to Tonia if she had refused to change?

- Celebrate changes within the family or classroom. Focus on the positive aspects.

- Encourage children to take small risks and praise them for trying, whether or not they are successful.

- Ask children what would be the worst thing that could happen if a reversible change is made. What would be the best possible result? Is it worth the risk?

- If a change is irreversible, help children think of and implement appropriate ways to deal with the situation.

- Assure children that it is normal to have fears or reservations about change, but stress that it is important not to let these fears limit their options in life.

- Be a role model. Embrace changes in your own life with enthusiasm.

- Ask children to list societal and technological changes that have improved people's lives (civil rights legislation, computers, organ transplants, etc.).

Welcome or not, change is one thing of which we can be sure. As the birds in the story told Tonia, it often feels like a free fall from a high nest. But what a heady feeling to discover that we can fly!

Sandy Stryker is co-author of the best selling *Choices: A Teen Woman's Journal for Self-awareness and Personal Planning; Challenges: A Young Man's Journal of Self-awareness and Personal Planning; Changes: A Woman's Journal for Self-awareness and Personal Planning;* and *More Choices: A Strategic Planning Guide for Mixing Career and Family.* This is her first children's book. She and her husband, Bill, live in St. Paul, Minnesota.

Itoko Maeno's earlier books for children include *Minou* by Mindy Bingham, *My Way Sally* by Mindy Bingham and Penelope Paine and *Kylie* by Patty Sheehan. Her illustrations of cosmopolitan Paris, the English countryside and the Australian outback are all accurate in detail, different in style and uniquely evocative of a particular place. Now, for *Tonia the Tree,* she has created a land of the imagination, an inviting and refreshing dream world in which all things are possible. Born in Tokyo, where she received a Bachelor's degree in graphic design, she has lived in the United States since 1982. Her work has been shown at the French Embassy in Washington, D.C., and has appeared in many other books.

Copies of this book may be ordered by sending $13.95 plus $1.50 shipping to *Tonia the Tree,* Advocacy Press, P.O. Box 236, Dept A, Santa Barbara, California 93102. (California residents add 6% sales tax.) Proceeds from the sale of this book will benefit the Girls Club of Santa Barbara, Inc., and contribute to the further development of programs for girls and young women.

Other books by Advocacy Press

Minou, written by Mindy Bingham, illustrated by Itoko Maeno. Hardcover with dust jacket, 64 pages with full color illustrations throughout. ISBN 0-911655-36-0. $12.95

My Way Sally, by Mindy Bingham and Penelope Paine, illustrated by Itoko Maeno. Hardcover with dust jacket, 48 pages with lovely color illustrations throughout. ISBN 0-911655-27-1. $13.95

Kylie's Song, by Patty Sheehan, illustrated by Itoko Maeno. Hardcover with dust jacket, 32 pages with full color illustrations throughout. ISBN 0-911655-19-0. $13.95

Father Gander Nursery Rhymes: The Equal Rhymes Amendment, by Father Gander. Hardcover with dust jacket, full color illustrations throughout, 48 pages. ISBN 0-911655-12-3. $12.95

Choices: A Teen Woman's Journal for Self-awareness and Personal Planning, by Mindy Bingham, Judy Edmondson and Sandy Stryker. Softcover, 240 pages. ISBN 0-911655-22-0. $14.95

Challenges: A Young Man's Journal for Self-awareness and Personal Planning, by Bingham, Edmondson and Stryker. Softcover, 240 pages. ISBN 0-911655-24-7. $14.95

More Choices: A Strategic Planning Guide for Mixing Career and Family, by Mindy Bingham and Sandy Stryker. Softcover, 240 pages. ISBN 0-911655-28-X. $15.95

Changes: A Woman's Journal for Self-awareness and Personal Planning, by Mindy Bingham, Sandy Stryker and Judy Edmondson. Softcover, 240 pages. ISBN 0-911655-40-9. $14.95

You can find these books at better bookstores. Or you may order them directly by sending a check for the amount shown above plus $1.50 each for shipping to Advocacy Press, P.O. Box 236, Dept. A, Santa Barbara, California 93102. For your review, we will be happy to send you more information on these publications.